Editor: Robert P. Arthur
Designer: Jeff Hewitt


San Francisco Bay Press
1671 39th Street
San Francisco, California 94122

SFP Paperback Edition
Library of Congress Cataloguing in
Publication Data

Shalaski, Ann: World Made of Glass

ISBN Number 978-1-60461-001-7

# World Made of Glass

To Sydney,
With all good wishes.
I hope you find joy in
World Made of Glass.

Love,
Ann Shalaski.
10/07

## Poems
### by Ann Falcone Shalaski

"For Ronnie, Ronda, Richard, and Cate"

# World Made of Glass

## Table of Contents

**Reflection**

**Sojourner**

# Passages

Grateful acknowledgment is made to the editors of the following magazines and journals in which some of these poems, several in earlier versions, first appeared:

*Beginnings:*
"Falling Into Place"

*ByLine:*
"Framed in White"

*Comstock Review:*
"Deep With Roots" and "Small Flowers"

*Endicott Review:*
"A Devil's Lark" and "Don't Ask Where I've Been"

*Natural Awakenings:*
"A Soft Place"

*Main Channel Voices:*
"Back In Stetsonville" and "You Again"

*New England Writers' Network:*
"Seeing Red"

*Poetry Society of Virginia 80th Anniversary Anthology of Poems:*
"At the Window"

*Port Folio Weekly:*
"Hershey Kisses and Elvis"

*Skipping Stones:*
"Sense of Direction"

*Virginia Adversaria:*
"Eggs Can Kill You"

*Meridian Anthology of Contemporary Poetry:*
"Connected" and "Under Gabled Windows"

Special thanks to Carolyn Kreither-Foronda, Nancy Powell, and Sofia Starnes, for showing me the way.

My gratitude as well, to Mike Correa, and Hollis Pruitt, whose work inspires me, and Bill Glose, my dear gifted, determined friend.

# Reflection

# Framed in White

We shovel our way down
the driveway, toss sparkling white
powder into the air. It reaches
the fence, towers in stacks, repeats
itself.

You remind me, "Everything can wait
but not this." I marvel at the motion
of your body, weight balanced
with purpose; scatter

rock salt that glitters
like rhinestone on pavement; see
the road map of the past.

My father, draped in frost, whistles,
clears wings of snow for my mother.
She traces a heart on the back porch
window, lifts a blue and white
cup of tea, knows that distance helps
to make things clear.

I find you, back at the beginning,
framed in white, watch
the way you turn, the way things turn
this first morning of winter,

the world made of glass.

## At the Window

How white the gulls in gray weather,
sky drained,
water dark, serious, waiting

for winter's shield to pull away,
one layer at a time. Breezes creep
like spirits across the bay.

Standing at the window,
I see my father preparing the cottage
for summer, scooping

white cloths from furniture, prying
nails from green-shuttered windows, pocketing
the shapeless fasteners.

My legs dangling,
curls doused with spray,
he carried me on his shoulders, walked

the water's edge zigzagging crazily.
Just enough sunlight for me to see
his footprints filling, forgotten until now.

# North Street

I was happy in the small neighborhood,
our home wedged between
the other two-story white houses.

Narrow driveways threaded
like ribbons to gardens bursting
with tomatoes, squash, and eggplants.

I rode my bike for salami
and bread past porches heavy
with honeysuckle vines.

My mother, waiting,
retraced her steps over
the worn linoleum floor

as the sewing machine stitched
dresses for me by a grandmother
who spoke no English,

planted jonquils turning
the afternoon air yellow,
tethering me to home.

# Don't Ask Where I've Been

The best part of being bad was knowing
I'd do it again.
Come home late,
creep up the stairs in stocking
feet, sweater sleeves flapping
like wings. Scarlet lipstick hidden
in my pocket.

Darkness softens sins when you're sixteen. Slipping
away like a rudder broken loose.  Running
past playgrounds, crossing
bridges of childhood.

While at the corner of midnight,
a mother waits to press
her hands to a daughter's face,
sweet, full of light.
Brush the cloud of hair falling
wild on her shoulders.

# Falling Into Place

I held my breath
and prayed for you
to grow, daughter,

asleep in a German featherbed
lent by strangers
to strangers.

You were born
pitifully small, with dark
eyes asking to be kept

and loved.  Shimmering
like glass,
a *kaleidoscope*

falling into place.
I cradled you with cupped
hands.

You soared, untethered,
circling wider and wider.
When I looked up,

you were grown.

# A Devil's Lark

Boys high five each other, search
for a perfect place to swim, float
at night in dark-oiled water
like angels among pilings.

No one would remember
what it was like to look down
without flinching, jump
from a rusty boat ramp, walk
on water, hands above heads,
fingers trailing loose as sea grass,
and disappear.

Sounds die first between heaven
and hell, sink from halo
of city lights, skyline projects, black
ash heaped by railroad cars.  Faces
at the altar of regret, white
as communion wafers, vanish.
Water closes, seals like a tomb,
baptizing its children
one by one.

# Filling Spaces

My father read Frost and Dickinson to me, played
minuets and waltzes before school in the morning.

Standing in the doorway,
he'd motion me on as I walked backwards,

keeping him in my gaze.  Bright yellow
dress dotted with white, lifting with each wave

of my arm.  Too soon, we laid him gently
into the earth, pillowing the ground with

marigolds, murmurs of prayers.  Year after year,
I find myself planting more golden anchors, filling

spaces, piecing together what I can remember:
shimmering ribbons of sounds,

words soaring from a voice rich,
lush as new gardenias.

A young girl waiting to bloom, listening,
as I do now, for her father.

# In the Kitchen

Sitting side by side,
women in my family

pass words, telling and retelling
stories as nimble fingers mend

socks on wooden eggs.
Perfect seams stitched into

pillowcases and aprons
from Monday's bleached flour sacks.

High-storied ceiling rings
with history:

births, deaths, frayed marriages,
the next generation scattering

like remnants underfoot.
I see them in dreams now,

tea seeping, soup cooling
on thick white plates, outline

of life spread on the bare
pine table like aged quilts sculpted

with dark blue ribbon.
They remind me

to repeat our family's story
because truth never ends.

It clings like pulled threads
not wanting to let go.

# Class Picture

I'm the one who doesn't know
what to do with her hands.
The one wearing her mother's pearls;
front row, third from the left.

I want to freeze-frame the moment,
stay suspended under glass
and never leave.
Never have to say I know

where I'm going,
or what my purpose is.
The others, so sure of themselves,
are eager to take off

when the shutter closes.
But I know nothing of beginnings,
distance from here to where I fit
in the universe.

So I concentrate, fold
my hands, search the lens
for a place, and I pretend
to smile.

# Gray Confusion

People don't sit on porches
anymore.  Hands on heads,
legs crossed at the ankles,

cooling themselves in the last folds
of evening.  No worn wicker chairs,
hanging baskets,

limp lazy cats curling
on wooden steps.  Neighbors gathering
before darkness thickens.

We rush in gray confusion, retreat
behind glass doors, overcrowded
highways at our backs.

No time to sit, think
about tomorrow, perch
on a railing, sun shining

like honey.  Or look into
the eyes of grandparents, find
what it is of them that's lasted.

Bodies motionless on porches,
sheltering oaks living
to be one hundred.

## Slow Drift of Time

Before summer exhaled its last breath,
I went back.  Saw the old house
where life began.  Swirling
outward in slow drift of time
like the swing chandeliered
to the front porch.

Followed the patterned path
set in shade where I spilled, scooped
jacks by twos and threes, believing
we would live forever.  Yellow
kitchen clock quietly ticking
years.

Driveway curves, turns past trees
I once climbed, sat perched,
certain someone would catch
me like a pear falling
in August.

Now, wild roses ramble
on the fence, follow their own design.
Stretch like children growing farther
and farther from sight.

Afternoon sun slipping,
I hear the whoosh of cars, house crumbling.
Voices thin as lines lift
from white lace curtains, come to me
like souvenirs.  Clear,
bright as a beginning.

# Sojourner

# Sense of Direction

*(For my grandfather, Salvatore Lucca, 1889-1971)*


How could you have been so sure
the sea, dark as your Sicilian wine,
would carry you to a new world?
Stream through continents, wind wrapped
around your shoulders.
Strapped suitcase strains with photographs,
memories sealed in starched new linen.
Hope bright as silver and gold pressed
to your chest.

When you knew nothing at all,
did you know something wonderful
would happen?
Home of your own, porch for scraping
boots, shaking mops, family dinners in
the kitchen every Sunday.
That you'd live your dream, never look back
at pier's edge or the rain beading
on your hat brim.

## Under Gabled Windows

he works the garden,
slow and gray;
snips wilted blossoms,
prized September roses unfurl;
tells me,
"Keep the front walk edged,
boxwoods topped,
back fence morning-gloried.
The best blackberries hang in high branches.
Remember how to fly."

His curled hands spade,
spread mounds of dirt
for dogwoods under gabled windows.
"Spring's not a sure thing," he says,
"and seasons slip quietly.
Make room for new growth."

# You Again

The problem is my mother doesn't know
who I am, what year it is.
She's forgotten that she loves rose
talcum and Tabu on her wrists, taught
me right from wrong, drilled weekly
spelling words into my head, nursed
me when I was sick.
It's as if she's never seen me before,
labors to say my name, tongue lost on
slick river of stones separating us.
I put soft felt slippers on her feet, tan
sweater over her shoulders and,
for a moment,
I think there's recognition in her eyes.
Or maybe it's the way light falls across
trees twisted and dying behind the house.

# It's Tuesday

Confused, she comes and goes
like a line drawn down
the highway.

Stops to search kitchen drawers,
bedroom closets crammed
with possessions for a sign,

something that will make sense
of her life.
A pale parasol, lips pursed

into wrinkled rings of thread,
my mother pulls words buried
like old roots, asking,

*What day is it?*
*What day is it?*
It's Tuesday, I tell her,

it's Tuesday.
As if the answer
could help.

# December Thirty-first

We circle midnight, swirl
in sequins, white tie and tails
black as a grand piano,

dance in someone else's darkness.
Promise to be perfect, thinner,
more ambitious,

know what to keep,
what to let go,
what makes us whole

as though turning a page
on the calendar will make us
new as a New Year's morning.

If only in that moment
shimmering like strips of tinsel,
one year passing

into another, we could wish
to be nothing more
than who we are.

# A New England Winter

begins in silence with little
fanfare.  Hard-angled world
made new, every tree and shrub
wrapped in linen.

Face pressed to kitchen window,
I seek shelter from the hourglass
of cold, watch sifting swirls dust
mailboxes, flower pots,

the front porch steps.
Snow shovel in hand, I trail
winter, leaving firm footprints
for spring to follow.

# April

Clothesline strung
from porch to pole,

I gather your shirts, hold
them close like years,

follow the garden path, shape
of your footprints.

April unfolds lilies,
forsythia bushes burst.

You clear branches, rake
flower beds,

plant my favorite pink
geraniums, call me honey.

I smile, lean like an old
fence post pressed to your chest.

Touch you like a delicate
bulb, satisfied.

## A Soft Place

Bold and wild,
arms spread wide as wings,
we navigate life on lids
of icy ponds,
cut patterns together. Circles
within circles, rings strong
as wedding bands.  Whirl
through years, wobble
a little as Earth turns on its axis
and mornings crack with frost.
Now,
winter weeps frozen,
you let go of my hand.  Pass,
thin as a blade, through pain, glide
on the edge of leaving.  Search
for a soft place
to fall.

# Push Back the Night

Every day you grow quieter,
thinner.  I count ribs like rings
of a tree,

tumor as big as your hand
once was.  Machines murmur,
breath crests and falls.

Undertow too strong
to surface, I know you'll leave.
Push back the night quiet

as a boat drifting
on water, break the line
between us, vanish

like a spirit weighted
with stones.  Life turning
on its side,

I move from chair
to chair, sit at the foot
of your bed, wondering,

What will become of me?
Like a sailor who wakes
when wind intrudes,

you stir,
eyes fixed on lights
at the edge of the world.

## No Stone Epitaph

There's a photo of you
and your father, faces turned
to one another.

A reminder of how strong a son
you were the day he asked to sit
by the window.

Slow-motion labor
to lift him from bed to chair,
pale slate of brow,

skeletal line of jaw,
faint smile when he sat, warm flush
on his face.

And I remember thinking,
let light claim him.
Let the afternoon's rays melt

ladder of bone
into gold leaves that drift
through sleep, vivid,

glowing.  When the sun sets,
and his absence
persists.

## Deep With Roots

Sorrow is my own yard
> where new grass never grows.

Flowers, fisted,
> sink into time.

Sadness scallops its paws,
> pushes me down in the same bed,

and the bones are yours.
> I pull on dying,

smell stars,
> approach God angry.

## Small Flowers

A psychic once told me,
spirits stand by my side waiting
to gather thoughts like small
flowers, putting them
in motion.

Surely then,
if I write your name in ink a thousand
times, fold it into paper wings,
you'll appear one morning,
like a bird on a fortunate wind.

# Edge of Day

Coffee cup in hand,
I pad noiselessly through tiled,
broom-cleaned kitchen,

hidden from a world rushing
like water over stones.
It feels right to begin the day

in this narrow space, quiet,
pure as a peach.
Go from window to window

as if they were parts of my life.
And I'm grateful for this calm
latitude, sacredness of light,

my own breath. Before the strangers
at my table speak with indifference,
tarnishing the morning.

## Connected

When I pass from this world,
I'll never just leave
and not return

to wander the long drive,
cathedral of weeping willows leading
to the house where I once lived,

French doors left open
like outstretched arms.
I'll see you doing what needs doing.

Laundry folded at the edge
of the bed, cats fed,
you'll close the blinds on the day's

dying, stand in that space
between here
and me.

# Passages

# Hershey Kisses and Elvis

It's as simple as this, I've been looking
for Elvis for fourteen years: on the airport
overpass, the Marriott reservation desk,
summer festivals where guitars conjure
foot tapping and gravel voices purge
private sorrows.
When someone said Elvis rented a one-bedroom
apartment on Pine Street near the Food Mart,
I stood in line for hours, certain he'd appear
from a pyramid of canned foods, flushed, in too-tight
suit. Hershey Kisses and peanut butter in his hands.
Sometimes I'm sure he's here. Stands in that place
between closed doors. Plays a riff, "Amazing Grace,"
soft, low. So I wait,
hold onto that look. Twitch snaking across
lips, spring-loaded thrust of his hips.
That nod from the King, head cocked sideways.

## Back in Stetsonville

Fat afternoon sun sinking,
the girls meet, sipping margaritas, green
as mint jelly.

No strangers to Ted's Tiki Bar, they sit
like Venus on the half-shell,
bright as neon lights.
Nails pearled,

legs waxed, yesterday's brides flirt
with men in pressed Khakis,
forgetting for a moment,
steady blare of football spiraling

from houses that need painting along
back roads where husbands, mud
on their jeans, wait for something to happen.
Good-old boys watching touchdowns

slip through fingers like empty years,
slow-moving dreams,
never knowing the score, time
running out.

New blonde hair falling on eyes frosted
blue as a jay's wing, prom queens perch
over drinks, retracing life's sharp turns,
how they were really meant for something

greater than making beds, biscuits,
knuckle-deep in dishwater.
If they could pick and choose again,
they'd marry a man that can kiss,

whisper words fragile as a January frost.
But this is Stetsonville,
and it's Saturday.
It's just Saturday.

# The Turning Time

My friends talk of recipes
and clothes, swirl ice in frosted
glasses, whisper of affairs.

Idle men are so divine,
they confide. I pause, toss
it all off with a braceleted wrist,

and as easily as breathing slip
into thoughts of you; coaxing
me down winding paths,

resurrecting me like a vintage
champagne. The improbability
bewildered me.

Such a feeling can only come
once. It's the turning time,
my friends say, sipping

white wine spritzers. Intoxicated,
I see you in everything, feel
the same flush of heat that passed

between us when I wrapped
myself around you, all too
ready, unbuttoned my blouse without

a care. The beauty is,
you'll soon forget.

## He's a Poet

pale as paper, face full
of lines.

Spends time writing
in his little black book,

poems women regret.  Stay
the night, ponder prose,

he tells them.  Paradise
is wordless.

# America's Sweetheart

Sometimes you forget,
Barbie was an ordinary woman
before cosmetic surgery.

Plump girl with a big shoe size,
spaces between her teeth.
Hair fried, dyed, parted

on the side, turned-down lips
no makeup could hide.
Before cellulite sucked from

her thighs like chocolate mousse
was recycled into her chest.
Crescent moon of chin lifted

from memory, smile permanently
etched.  Sometimes you forget
a beauty queen lives in a glass

box, eats wheat toast and black
coffee, senses dulled.
That you weren't meant to wear

shiny tight pants, stretch-lace
body suits, or hear high heels trill
like castanets on the kitchen floor.

That being perfect is not
what you think it is,
and even hours give you away.

# Mall Miracles

Blondes dressed in black, scented
orchid blossoms behind earlobes,
hands smooth with almond oil,

work the cosmetic counters, skirt
edges of glass for faces folding
like fans.

Weathered landscapes in need
of creamy pink lotions,
elixirs of youth in tiny vials.

Eyes sparkle, skin glows, perfume
swells as sleek cygnets
in ebony coats, glide

on escalators going up.
Swirl past the swan in me
going down.

# Seeing Red

I try not to notice
when you look at another woman,
smiling,

eyes poring over her body,
the way you looked at me
the first time,

your face flushed crimson,
blood surging.
The same look

makes me see red,
sip
burgundy sangrias.

## Something About a Wedding

makes me want to rescue
the bride and groom teetering
on a three-tiered cake, hoping

for love to catch.  Everlasting bliss
following like a string
of pearls.

It's flowers arranged like promises,
photos out of focus.
Bride's lace and satin against

rosebud peaks of breasts, groom whispering
in her ear that makes me want to collect
words scattered like rice, replay

them on nights when silence
is a fringed canopy over the bed.
It's the slow waltz over mountains

made from molehills, losing a diamond,
one syllable at a time,
that makes me inch backwards.

Bouquet of lilies sails
over open hands.

## Pale Pink

I bought heart-shaped pillows
trimmed in lace, painted
the bedroom pink,

believed him.
He brought roses, spread
petals blood red,

covering me in promises
sweet enough to swallow,
but never took me home

to mother, or left his wife.
I sleep where the contours
of his body remain,

on sheets pale pink,
the color of roses
washed away.

# Twist of Lime

I remember the night we had
Mexican food.  Green chilies sizzle
on porcelain plates,

salty margaritas, smooth as river
rocks.  Ceiling fans stir
the amber air,

a man at the bar neatly stacks
empties.  Guitars strum,
you slow dance me through

leaving, hum that no one
stays together for long.
I think of you summer nights,

pass the open door of the restaurant,
legs bare, tomato red lipstick.
Cotton soft skirt flaring.

# Life, So Far

Don't talk to me about love,
or try to tempt me with
quick witty lines,

eyes that shine sex.
Even I know life is too short
for a woman to work through

a man's troubles, fake addresses,
flashy bills.  Days and months turn
into years of disappointments.

I'd rather be single than settle
for the kind who swaggers, smiles,
seduces a woman,

leaves her crying, unraveled
like a twelve-car pile-up
on a foggy morning.

So don't talk love
to me, I've tasted you. Traced
your long lean latitude

until my heart dissolves.
Played in your fire, softening.
I won't listen,

because loving is hard,
and leaving
is worse.

## This is Perfection

Being on the edge is better.
Misery from a distance resembles beauty.

The cold world hisses,
ice beads and freezes
the moon on windows.  Dreams dry
on mats by metal doors
where Jesus, sheltered
behind glass, arms raised,
surrenders to neglect.

Love is currency
because we have made it so.

Skirts are hiked higher.
Boys become fathers pushing
babies in carriages through
gunpowder blue horizons,
black pavements turning
to gravel.

The mind lets go,
we forget,

sorrow drops through spokes
like marbles rolling
into infinity.  No one weeps.
Everyone expects to walk
backwards, put some spin
on it.  Play dead.

Who would have thought
it could be so easy?

# Ode to Elvis

I wrote his name
in colored pencils across
my notebook, taped

his picture to my bedroom
wall.  Studied the glossy black
sweep of hair,

dark liquid eyes, hypnotic smile.
Heard the brush and drag
of his fingers across the guitar,

that low guttural growl,
and I loved him.  Tenderly kissed
his picture,

our lips touching like a teacup
in a saucer.  One Sunday,
I saw him on TV,

head thrown back, body pulsating,
hips writhing.
My heart pounding,

I put his name in metal
studs across my jacket,
*Elvis…forever.*

# Play, Makeup, and Clothes

I want to be like Barbie, flexible,
with knees that bend,
a twelve-inch waist and a shapely
rear end.

I'd trade my limbs, they're in slow
decline, for those long toned
legs and I'll gift her
mine.

I'll tan by her pool, practice posing
just right, bleach my gray
hair blonde and stay out
all night.

Barbie can have my life,
cook and iron for no pay,
feed the dog, find the cat,
have my kind of day.

It's time she faced reality:
an older princess doll
is moving in, and it happens
to be me.

I'm going to wear her red shoes,
go on a date with Ken, have sex
in Barbie's pink bed,
change outfits, and do it again!

# Eggs Can Kill You

I measure my intake
and record every gram.
I follow nutritional guidelines,
my menu is well planned.

Salt is a no, no.
Sugar is out.
Red meat is forbidden,
butter and cream can lead to gout.

I've eaten dried geraniums,
and tofu patties, too.
I've simmered raw cabbage
and consumed the smelly brew.

I've read that eggs can kill you,
pork is taboo.
Fish are swimming in kepone.
What is a person to do?

I am tired of the confusion,
the frantic worry and doubt.
I have decided to eat the things I like,
the foods I have done without.

I'll start with a donut,
jelly squishy and red,
a latte for dunking,
chunky peanut butter on bread.

I won't forget my calcium,
dairy products will do.
Double dips of ice cream, please,
and an Almond Joy, or two.

This is a marvelous idea,
try it, do as I do.
Take big yummy bites of everything,
and spit before you chew.

# Real Women

I've had it with all the thin
joggers lank as wheat.
Long-legged Lizzies
who seldom eat.

Spandex junkies
wherever I turn.  Fitness
fanatics with energy
to burn.

Boy-shaped sisters jumping
up and down.  No clue
at all that there's a shape
called *round*.

Real women sag, bag,
don't own exercise machines.
We're plump as mushrooms,
and we'll never be lean.

We come in all sizes,
some short, some tall.
Real women age overnight,
cellulite and all.

We don't touch our toes,
extreme makeovers won't do.
We like who we are,
real women, that's who.

# Men

I like young men
so firm and so fresh,
muscular thighs,
and no sagging flesh.

Chins that are chiseled,
ribs you can feel,
hair that's not graying,
teeth that are real.

Biceps rippling,
eyes eager and bright,
no naps at midday,
they're up all night.

Sculptured bodies
bronzed by the sun,
delicious and tempting,
I really like men,
                young.

## Sign Here

I'm in love
with the UPS man
in brown shorts,
firm thighs.

Study his movements
through the blinds, flex
of flesh under his shirt,
clipboard pressed
to a trim waist,
package in capable hands.

"Sign here," he tells me
as I take his pen, trade
smiles.  Watch his lips move
up and down, soft smooth
surface of skin.

Secretly wishing
I had shaved my legs,
put on lipstick,
could film the whole scene again
and again.

Where he approaches my door
naked,
and he isn't in a hurry.

# Almost Famous

I suppose it's not too late
to be famous.  Trade clogs
and faded jeans for suits, silk
blouses with bits of beading
to wear at book signings.

Publishers and editors will court me, demand
the impossible.  I'll be exhausted stacking
syllables, striking adverbs from scaffold of scribbled
scraps.  Building towers of metaphors, graceful
as dolphins turning cartwheels in an arc.

Sometimes, I'll just have to stop, listen
to country music, sit on my plush red
couch.  Collage of small black letters tumbling
in mid-sentence, adjectives and line-breaks
where I leave them.

I'll collect stacks of outlines stored
in files, find my glasses, say
what I want to say.  A few nouns here,
a spectacular verb there, words pouring
in waves.

I'll use all the new shiny felt-tipped
pens on my desk,
the ones that'll make me famous.
At readings,
I'll greet old friends,

student poets lined end to end
like parked cars.  Waiting for a smile,
or a few witty words from me, enjambed,
of course. They'll lean forward,
slowly spell first and last names

as my hand flits across the title page
of the ninth in a series of twenty-four
poetry books.
And I'll remember to tell them,
good luck with your writing.

## About the Author

Ann Shalaski was born in Connecticut and lives in Newport News, Virginia. A member of The National League of American Pen Women and the Poetry Society of Virginia, she is president of the advisory council for Christopher Newport University's Writers' Conference and Writing Contest. She is a workshop presenter and hosts monthly open mic poetry events.

An award-winning poet and a short story writer, her story of a family's disconnect and rivalry appears in *Keeper of the Stories, A Guide to Writing Family Stories*. Ms. Shalaski's poems have appeared in *The Comstock Review, Main Channel Voices, Port Folio Weekly, ByLine,* and numerous other publications.

984684